P9-CQE-769

THE MATCHBOX DIARY

For Ethan, Simon, Oliver, and Charlie
P. F.

First edition 2013

Library of Congress Catalog Card Number 2012942613
ISBN 978-0-7636-4601-1

13 14 15 16 17 LEO 10 9 8 7 6 5 4 3

Printed in Heshan, Guangdong, China

This book was typeset in Cheltenham.
The illustrations were done in acrylic gouache.

Candlewick Press
99 Dover Street
Somerville, Massachusetts 02144

visit us at www.candlewick.com

PAUL FLEISCHMAN

ILLUSTRATED BY **BAGRAM IBATOULLINE**

CANDLEWICK PRESS

Pick whatever you like the most. Then I'll tell you its story."

"There's so many things here."

"You'll know when you see it. And then I'll know something about you. The great-granddaughter I've only heard about."

"So. You like boxes, just like me. You smoke cigars?"

"No."

"Me, either. There's no cigars in it, anyway."

"What's inside?"

"Not just one story, but lots."

"What's in the little boxes?"

"My diary."

"What's a diary?"

"A way to remember what happens to you. Usually it's a book people write in. When I was your age, I had a lot I wanted to remember, but I couldn't read or write. So I started this. Open the first one."

La Luna
BRYANT & MAY'S
SPECIAL SAFETY MATCH
IL LEOPARDO
FIAMMIFERI
SAFETY MATCHES
MADE AT BERGEN NORWAY
LOCOMOTIVE
BRYANT & MAY'S
RUBY MATCHES
THE CHAMPION
TRADE MARK
PARAFFIN MATCH
SICUREZZA
ACCENDIBILI
FIAMMIFERI
50
HALDEN'S
TELEPHONE
ELECTRIC
LIGHTS
MATCHES
MARCA DI FABBRICA
THE LANCER
SAFETY MATCHES
MADE IN AUSTRALIA
ENGLAND
KNIGHT
BROTHERS, L'D
PAMPA
IN THE WORLD
BEST
BIRD BRAND
MORELANDS
SPECIAL
BRITISH MADE
SAFETY MATCHES

"What is it?"

"An olive pit. I put it in my palm, and I'm right back in Italy. That's where I grew up. Lots of olive trees there. Life was hard — the other reason I saved it. No floor in our house, just dirt. No heat in winter except the fire under the cooking pot. And sometimes not enough food. When I'd tell my mother I was hungry, she'd give me an olive pit to suck on. It helped."

"Who's this?"

"My father—he went to America to work. He sent money home. Lots of Italian men did. I was a baby when he left. All I remembered about him was his mustache. Once he sent pictures so we wouldn't forget him.

"My father never went to school. Back then, most kids had to help their parents all day. He had to get someone to write his letters home from America. When one came, we had a problem. Four older sisters, my mother, and me. None of us could read. We had to take it to the schoolmaster.

"He had a son, older than me, who could read and write."

"Every day that boy wrote down what happened in a diary. Every year he got a new one. Red leather, with a silk bookmark. I had no idea how to write, but I was wild to have my own diary."

"I want one, too."

"That's my girl."

“There was a year with no rain. No wheat. No macaroni. The schoolmaster wrote a letter to my father for us. We waited. A long time later, a letter came back, with tickets to sail to America. When we left, my grandmother cried in the road. ‘You’ll eat the food there and forget your home!’ Over and over.”

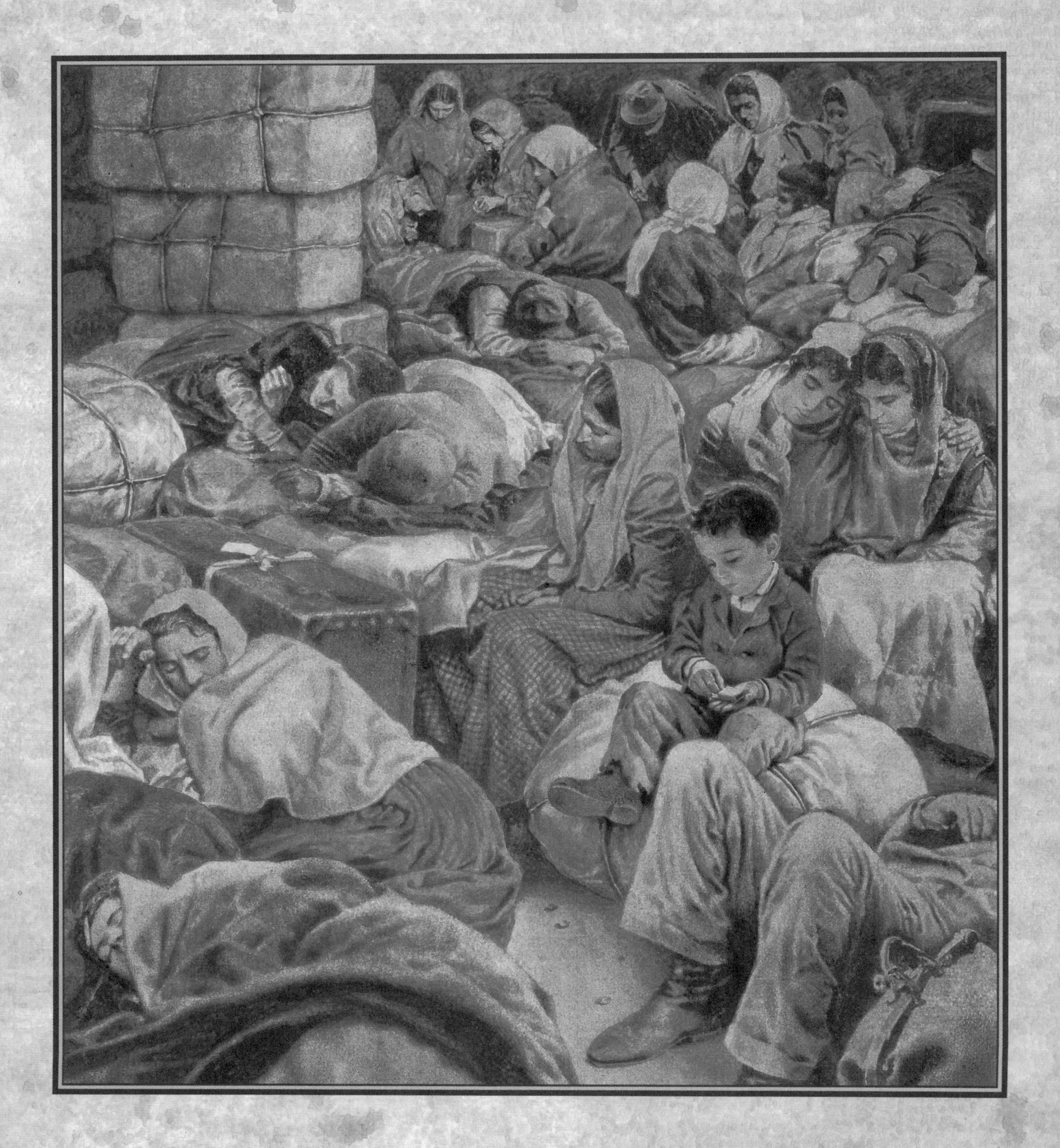

“We took a horse-drawn carriage to Naples. It was the first time I’d seen a car. And drinks in bottles. And the ocean. We slept three nights on the floor in the steamship station, waiting for our boat. That’s where I found the matchboxes. I’d told my grandmother I wouldn’t forget her or anything else. That’s when I started the diary.”

“Our ship left. We were in the bottom, where the motion was worst. People seasick, moaning. My sisters took me up on deck. You like that hairpin? When I found it, I looked up, and high above us were rich ladies in big hats on the upper decks. People said there was gold lying on the ground in America. I thought my mother and sisters would look like those women soon.”

“We were headed for Ellis Island, in New York. Someone told me that men would stick buttonhooks in our eyes there.”

“What’s a buttonhook?”

“A metal tool for closing up shoes, before there were laces. I had nightmares about the buttonhook men. Then we had bigger problems. A storm hit us. Maybe a hurricane. The boat bucked like a horse. I saw a bunch of the sailors praying together. Not good. Saint Christopher is supposed to protect travelers. People threw medallions of him in the ocean, begging him to spare us. After three days, the water calmed.”

"How long did it take you to fly across the country? Five hours? That trip from Italy took nineteen days. I know because I put a sunflower seed shell in this box every morning. Then everyone was calling, *'La Statua della Libertà!'* I ran up to the deck. There was New York. A boat came up to ours, selling food. Our neighbors on the ship bought bananas and gave my family one. I bit into it and spat it out. I didn't know you're supposed to peel it."

"How come this one's empty?"

"I'll tell you why. We got off on Ellis Island. They didn't want to let in anybody sick, especially people with eye diseases. All morning I'd been crying because of the buttonhook man. When I saw him, I screamed. He grabbed me and used the handle to roll up my eyelid and look underneath. 'Red,' he said. 'He can't come in.' My mother fainted. My oldest sister found a doctor who spoke Italian and told him my eyes were red from crying. She gave me peppermint candies to calm me down. Later, a new doctor checked me, using his finger. That one let me pass. I put a candy in the box. Then the next week I ate it."

"My father met us. Everyone cried. I smelled his mustache to see if it was really him.

"We took a boat to New York, then a train somewhere else. The next day, we started work in the canneries. All seven of us. Cutting fish all day, always a man watching to make sure we weren't slowing down. They gave us old falling-apart sheds to live in, as crowded as the ship."

"You didn't have your own room?"

"No, sweetheart."

"Canning fish. Sorting peaches. Shelling peas. Then down to the South, peeling shrimp and opening oyster shells. Wherever there was work. We moved so often, I could barely remember where I was or where I'd been. That's why I started saving bits of newspapers, so that someday I could look back and say I was in that exact place on that exact day. I still love newspapers."

EASTCOAST CANNING CO.
132 MILE

"Instead of jewels, my mother and sisters had fish scales on their arms. The strange thing was, when we walked down a street and maybe passed a grocery, the same people who bought our cans of sardines wouldn't look at us. Back then, some people didn't want Italians here. Sometimes boys threw rocks. That's how my tooth got here."

SHIPYARD
WAREHOUSE

"That's my favorite box. My first baseball game. I didn't understand it, why the men were running. But I was in heaven not to be working and to sit by my father. Under the grandstands I found more matchboxes. Then, in a clump of grass, a quarter. That meant we could go again. To me, it seemed like one of the lumps of gold people said we'd find."

“I think I was eight when we got an apartment and all rolled cigars at the kitchen table. A few years later we switched to shelling nuts for restaurants, day and night. Then my father got hired at a foundry in Pittsburgh, making railroad parts. My sisters sewed in a factory. My mother told my father I should go to school. She’d seen me staring at signs and circus posters, trying to understand. Sometimes I’d draw letters with a piece of coal. She wanted me to learn and teach my sisters. Big argument. Days and weeks.”

CIRCUS

"Who won the argument?"

"I'll give you a hint. I went to school. It was hard. English seemed as crazy as baseball. I had to sit with the little kids. They made fun of how I talked, but I learned to read and write. What they taught us during the day, I taught my sisters that night. Then I went to a different school where I learned typesetting—picking out the lead letters from their compartments. That's how everything was printed before computers. I had good eyes from always looking for little things for my matchboxes. I became a printer."

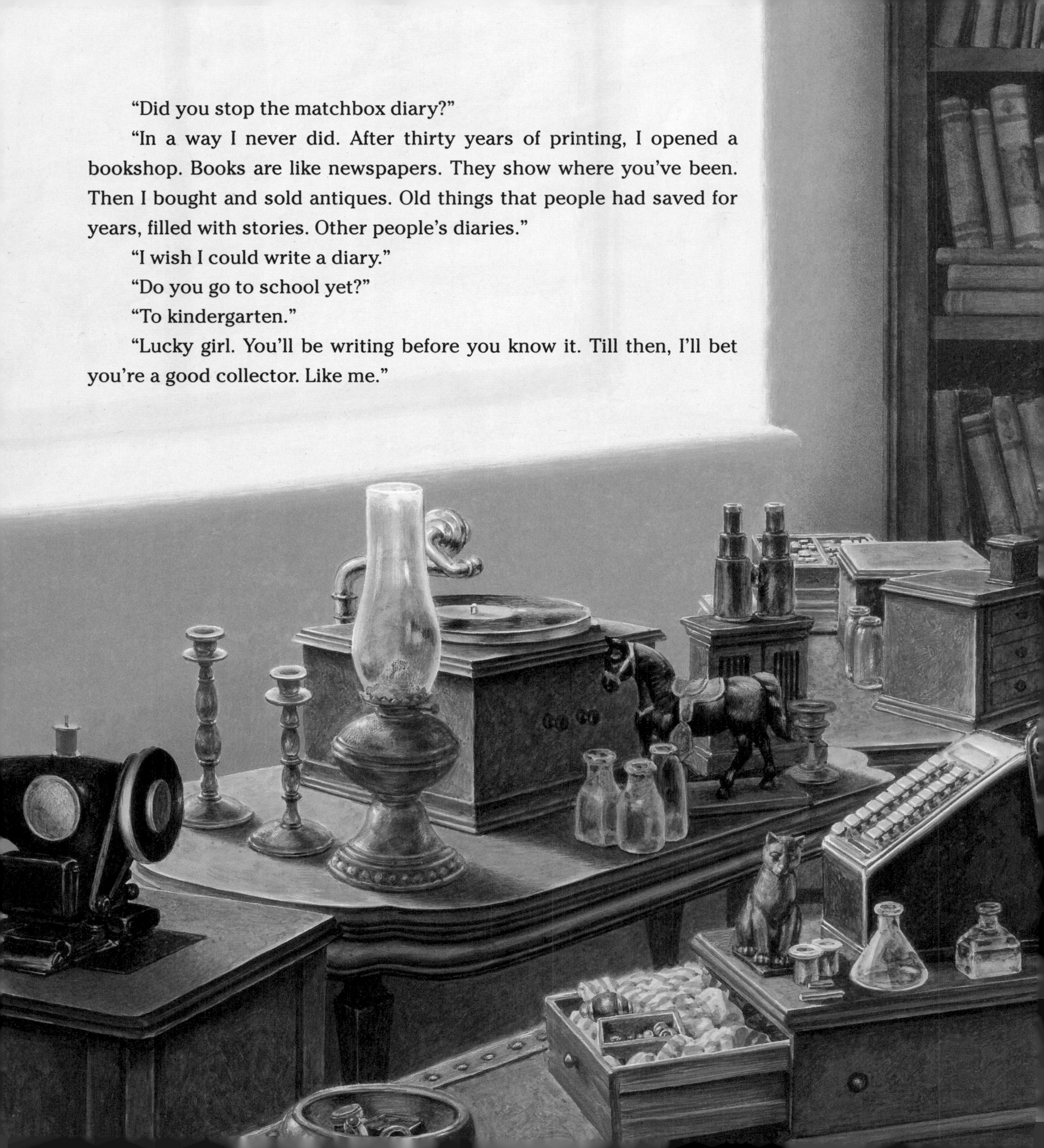

"Did you stop the matchbox diary?"

"In a way I never did. After thirty years of printing, I opened a bookshop. Books are like newspapers. They show where you've been. Then I bought and sold antiques. Old things that people had saved for years, filled with stories. Other people's diaries."

"I wish I could write a diary."

"Do you go to school yet?"

"To kindergarten."

"Lucky girl. You'll be writing before you know it. Till then, I'll bet you're a good collector. Like me."

Candies